JRc

17 JUL 2015

For Susan
—M. I. B.

For my dad, always young at heart
—D. R. O.

ACKNOWLEDGMENTS
The illustrator thanks Justin Chanda, Laurent Linn, and Dani Young at
Simon & Schuster Children's for helping to make the creative process so much FUN.

SIMON AND SCHUSTER
First published in Great Britain in 2014 by Simon and Schuster UK Ltd
1st Floor, 222 Gray's Inn Road, London, WC1X 8HB
A CBS Company

Originally published as 'Naked' in 2014 by Simon and Schuster Books for Young Readers,
an imprint of Simon and Schuster Children's Publishing Division, New York

A CIP catalogue record for this book is available from the British Library upon request

ISBN: 978-1-4711-2244-6 (PB)

Printed in China

2 4 6 8 10 9 7 5 3 1

www.simonandschuster.co.uk

Who Needs PANTS?

Michael Ian Black

ILLUSTRATED BY

Debbie Ridpath Ohi

SIMON AND SCHUSTER

New York   London   Toronto   Sydney   New Delhi

Look at me, everybody!

I'm naked!

Running around

naked!

Sliding down the stairs

naked!

Eating a **cookie** totally and completely naked!

I should dress like
this **all** the time.

I could go to school **naked.**

Play at the playground **naked.**

Do the hokey-cokey **naked.**

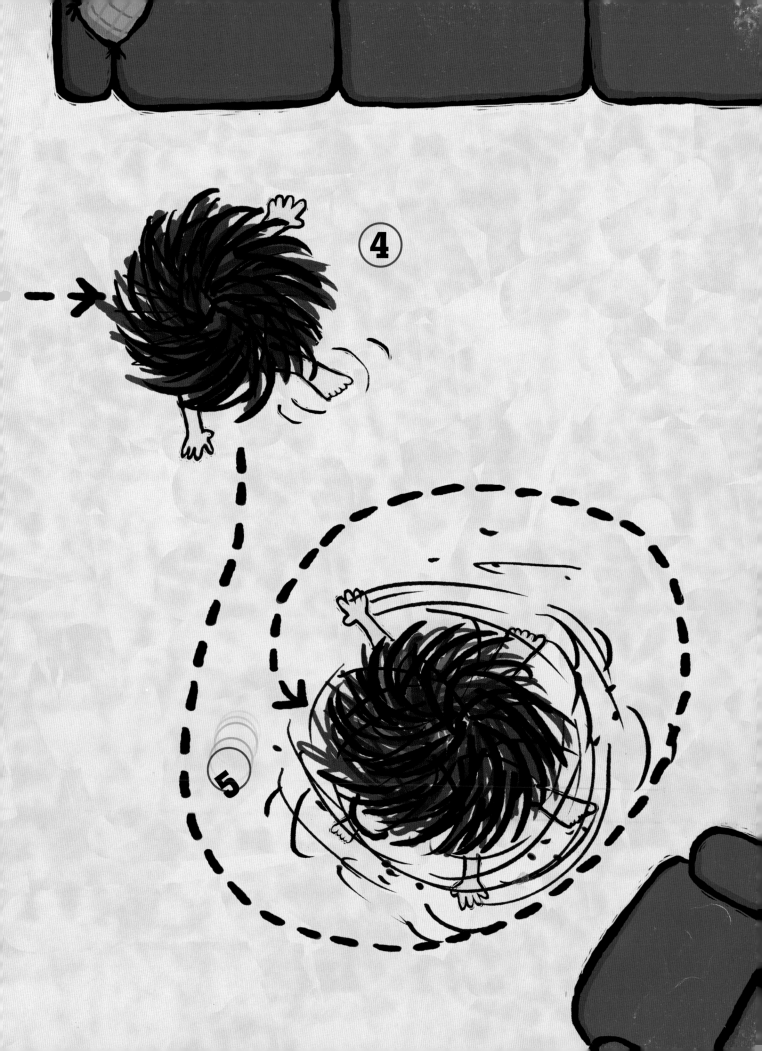

Pants?

Who needs pants?

Or shirts

or shoes

or capes.

Fighting evildoers

caped!

bad guys' HeadQuarters

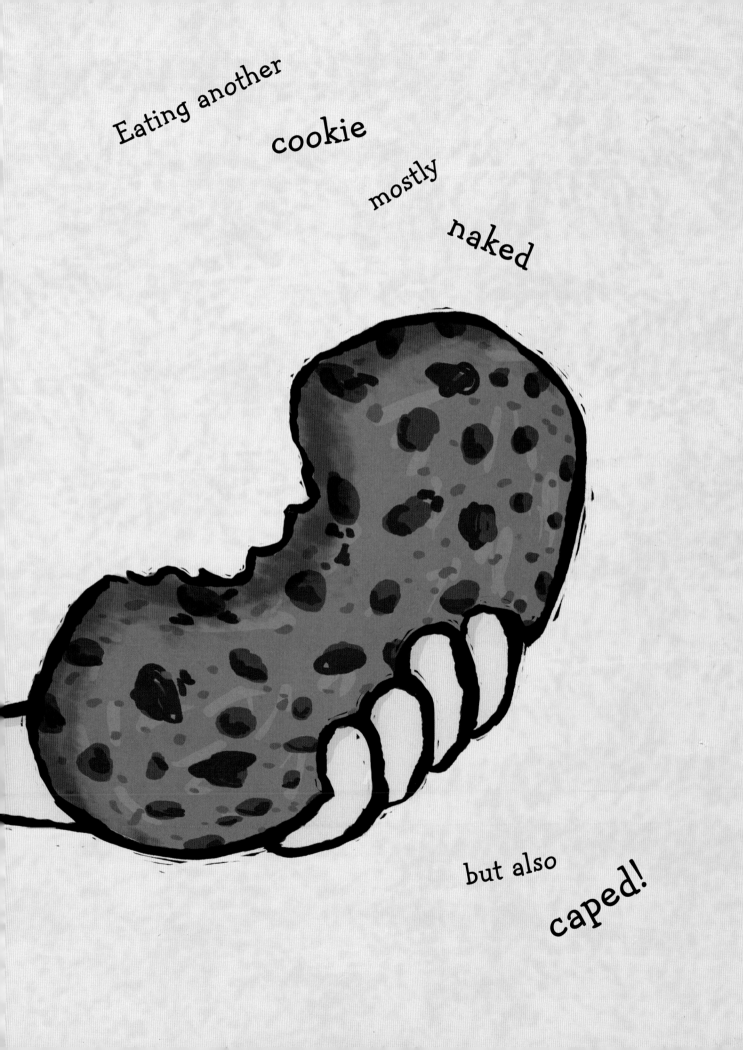

Being naked is great,

but being

caped

is even

better!

Except that now I'm . . .

Sneaking

downstairs

cold.

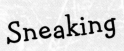

Eating one last cookie

cold.

Maybe I should put on some pyjamas.

And a top.

And maybe these slippers.

And maybe take off the cape.

And now I am . . .

exhausted.

And now I am . . .

asleep.